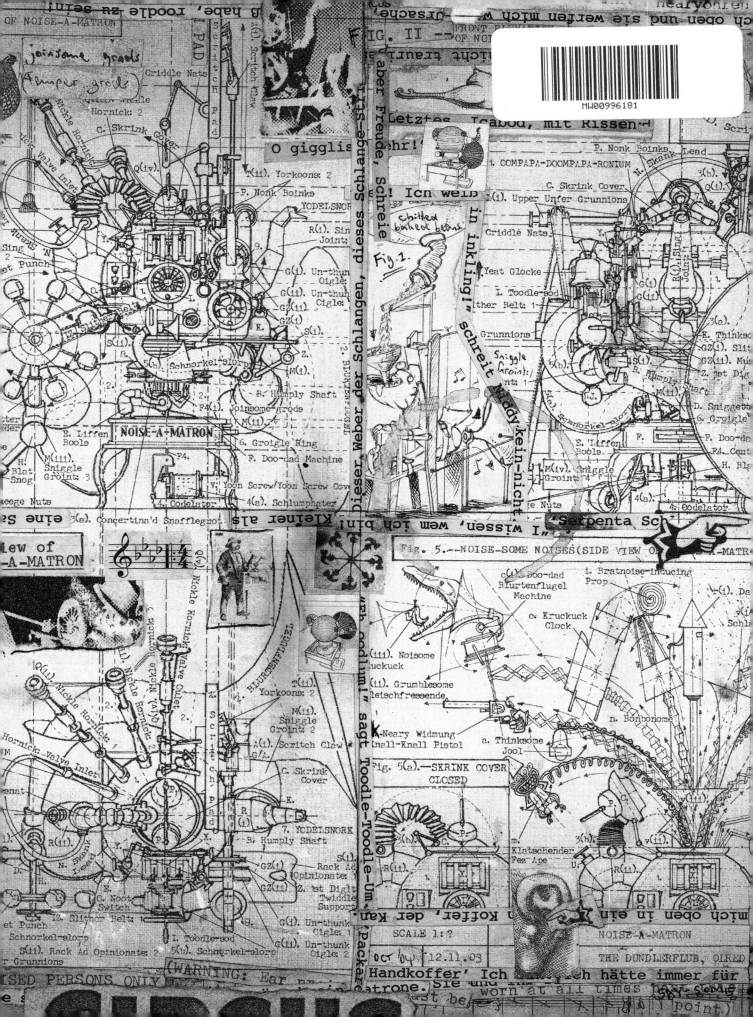

for KERRY NEARY!
★★★★

KNICK-NIDDLING
DISINCLINATIONARY
ABSTRACTS:

Originally published in hardcover in Australia by Lothian Books.

www.houghtonmifflinbooks.com

The text of this book is set in Filosofia.
The illustrations were done in oils, ink, and collage.

Library of Congress Cataloging-in-Publication Data
Svendsen, Mark Nestor, 1962–
Circus Carnivore / written by Mark Svendsen ; illustrated by Ben Redlich.
p. cm.
Summary: In rhyming nonsense verse, a young girl explains how the
creatures who live in her head affect her behavior.
ISBN-13: 978-0-618-56328-9 (hardcover) ISBN-10: 0-618-56328-8 (hardcover)
[1. Behavior—Fiction. 2. Monsters—Fiction. 3. Stories in rhyme.]
I. Redlich, Ben, ill. II. Title.
PZ8.3.S99214Cir 2006   [Fic]—dc22   2006004791

Manufactured in China
LEO 10 9 8 7 6 5 4 3 2 1

The ILLUSTRATOR acknowledges the
QUEENSLAND GOVERNMENT
for financial ASSISTANCE through ARTS Queensland.

Queensland Government
Arts Queensland

Fig. 5.—NOISE-SOME NOISES

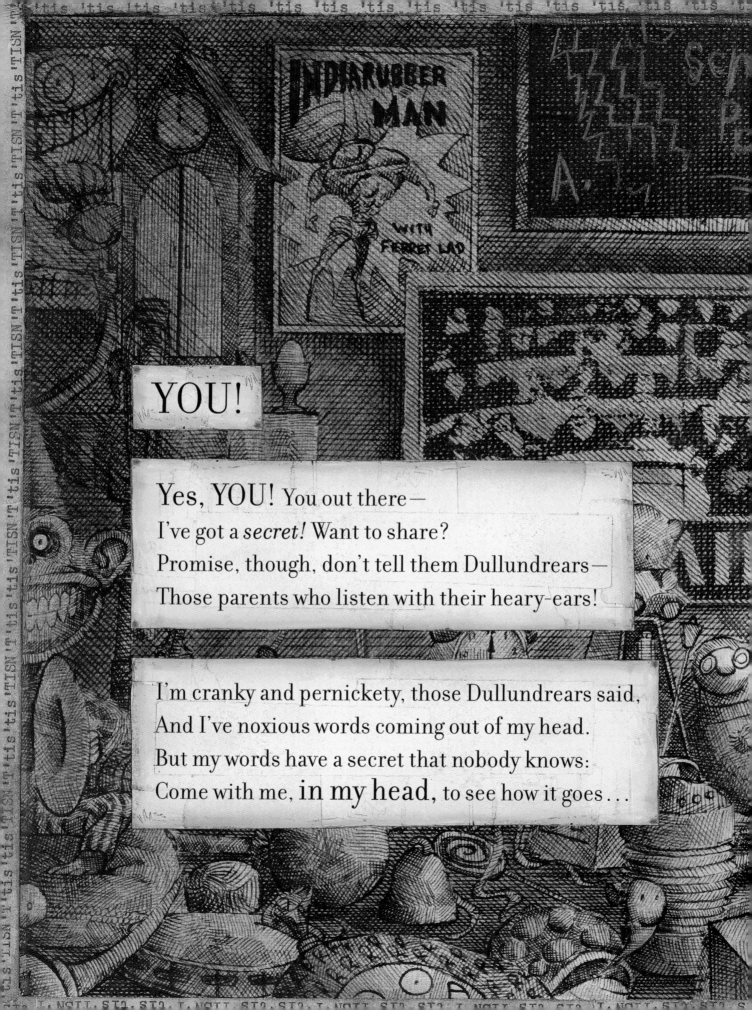

YOU!

Yes, YOU! You out there—
I've got a *secret!* Want to share?
Promise, though, don't tell them Dullundrears—
Those parents who listen with their heary-ears!

I'm cranky and pernickety, those Dullundrears said,
And I've noxious words coming out of my head.
But my words have a secret that nobody knows:
Come with me, in my head, to see how it goes...

They think when I spurtle noise-some words
That I thought, then chose to say them;
But my words all come from my noise-a-matron—
Say hello to the people who make them.

Noolman there works the liffin bools,
For screeching out my groigles,

While Tubswort toils on the doo-dad machine,
That stamps my niggly foibles.

Toodle-Um and Niddy-no-not
Both hurl my un-thunk oigles,

And not forgetting our Icabod,
Who turns the winsome toodle-sod
That makes my noise-some noises.

You want to know where they live, these sods?
They live beside my temper grods, inside my think-some noodle.

Das die winsome Toodlegrasscholle dreht,

And they make whatever noise they choose
To show the world I've got the blues, whenever I won't be *goodle!*

Those Dullundrears,
     they work that way:
They say I can't enjoy my play,
They pack me up
     and they throw me away,
'Cause I'm having fun being *roodle*!

IARUBBER
MAN

WITH
FERRE LAD

DALMER

CADMIUM
RED DEEP
(HUE)

NiosE
pROgr
ORTHAR;
PetSup
DWnly

O sad be the wince,
O shriven the pride.
O sorrow the wretch,
O haughtless the slide.

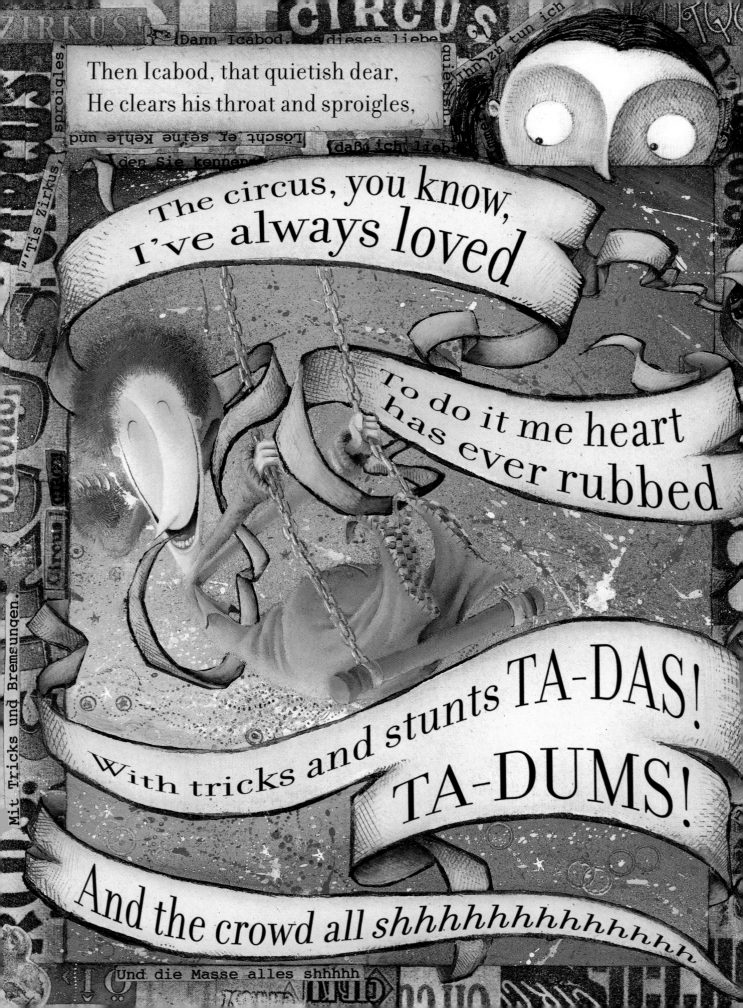

then NOISAL!

About it Noolman sits to think, as Tubswort turns to Toodle,
Who turns in turn to Niddy-no-not, who scratches on her noodle.

But startling-up,
our Olred cries,

With flub I's done!

With Dundling too!

I'll make up a circus with Icabod.
I'll ringling rings and I'll barnum-bod.

I'm

PANDEMONIUM

VON BELLOW

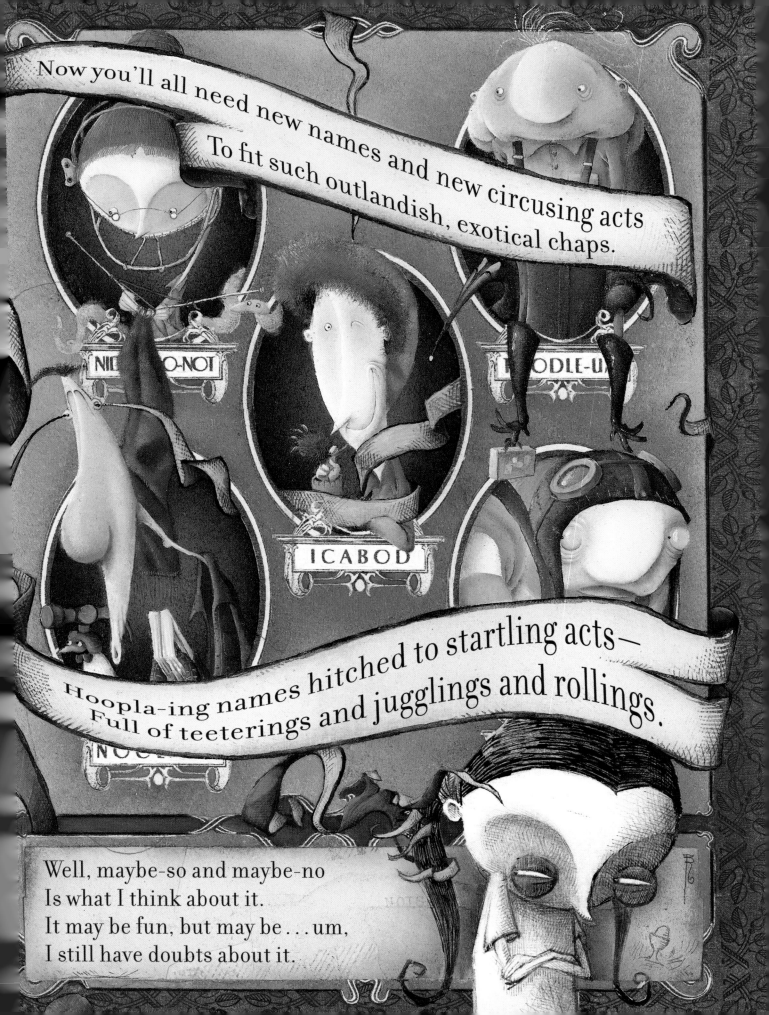

Now you'll all need new names and new circusing acts
To fit such outlandish, exotical chaps.

NI[D]...O-NOT

ICABOD

[D]OODLE-U...

Hoopla-ing names hitched to startling acts—
Full of teeterings and jugglings and rollings.

NO[...

Well, maybe-so and maybe-no
Is what I think about it.
It may be fun, but may be ... um,
I still have doubts about it.

Then
Noolman cries,

I's got an act!

An act
I's got for me!

CORMACK McCALLUM:
CHOOK BALANCER

That's who I wants to be!

Next Tubswort calls,
And I'm warminup!
Here's what me act will be and all—
I'll be DEVIL-MAY-CARE
JETSON D'ANGLETERRE
THE HUMAN CANNONBALL

Hey! I know in an inkling!

cries Niddy-no-not.

I know who I'll be!

THAT WEAVER OF SERPENTS
THAT SNAKE-KNITTING BABE

SERPENTA

Snake Wrangler

that's me!

Eh oodlum! says Toodle-Um.

Packard Portmanteau

I am!

$14.

I've always wanted, forever, to be

THE CONCERTINA'D MAN

I'll fold myself up in a tiny suitcase,
Smaller than a sardine can.

Last, Icabod, with tears in his eyes,
Tears not of sad, but of joy, cries,

And I'm

GARGLE McSNEEZE
ON
THE FLYING TRAPEZE

I'm a laughs-aloud clown
And I'm joysomely pleased
To delight all the crowds
with me gladden!

O tiddle me wink!

O chuckle guffaw!

O winslowing whoopie!

O gigglish more!

You may think when I spurtle JOY-SOME words

That I laughed, then chose to say them;

But my words are made in the

CIRCUS CARNIVORE,

Where they teeter and trip and acts up more,

With tricks and stunts

CIRCUS
CARNIVORE

and laughs galore

DANKSAGUNG

FräulEin Kate O'SullivaN, Elena Kats-CherniN, Helen ChamberliN, Dover PublicatioNs NY, Carmel McMurrey und — Mit ewiger DaNkbarkeit

Circus Campire

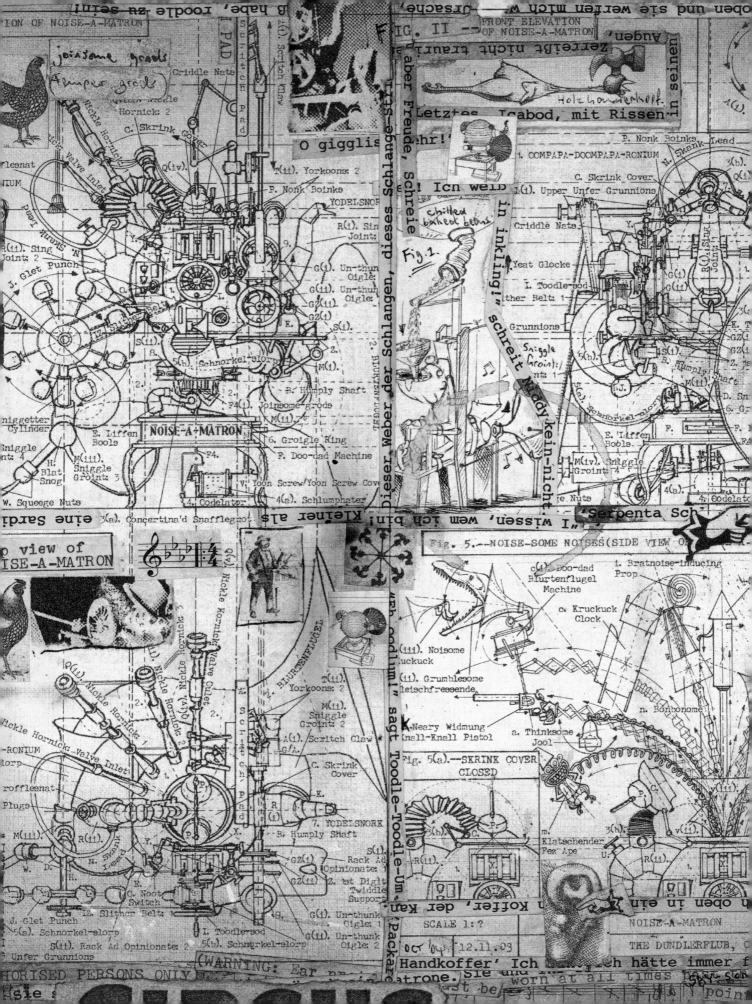